May Kokopelli
Put a Smile in
Your Heart!

———————— Tom Boulton

The First Kokopelli ™

Dedicated to Deb, Chris, and Ben

The First Kokopelli
Copyright 2014

ISBN 978-1-63068-426-6

Manufactured in the United States
First Printing March 2014

Bang Printing, 3323 Oak Street, Brainerd, MN 56401

Little Fox was an Indian boy. He and his family were members of a small tribe that lived in the desert. They survived by growing corn and other vegetables, by gathering wild plants and seeds, and by hunting.

Like all Indian boys, Little Fox loved to hunt.
And he worked in the fields when he was told.

Other times he helped his
Grandfather make and repair tools.

One day, when Grandfather was caught up with his work, he said to Little Fox,
"Today I will make you something. What would you like?"
"A flute!" the boy blurted out. Little Fox loved music and dancing.
With a flute he could learn to play a tune!
"Fine," said Grandfather. "Bring me the leg bone of
a large bird and I will make you a fine flute."
These bones were easy to work because they were
hollow and light.

An eagle or turkey would be best. Eagles had fine feathers and turkey meat was delicious. But it was impossible to sneak up on eagles, and turkeys were hard to find. Why not a buzzard? They were large and Little Fox thought he might have a way to get one. A few days later he begged meat scraps from a woman who was scraping down an animal hide.

The next day, Little Fox climbed up high in some rocks and, in an open space, spread out the scraps.

He hid with his bow and arrows.
The smell of the meat soon brought buzzards.
Little Fox smiled at the circling birds, but had
to wait for them to land. Just when he felt
he couldn't stay still another moment,
the birds settled and began to feed.
Silently he drew back his bow and…

GOT one!
He grabbed it and held on tight, even though he feared the wounded buzzard might fly off with him. Finally, the bird gave up.

He proudly showed the buzzard to his mother. She offered to cook it if he cleaned it. He did and saved the tail feathers, for they were large and might be of some use.

The meat was tough and stringy.
Even so, cooked in a stew with wild onions, it was a meal that filled everyone up.
As they ate, Grandfather fished a long bone from the pot and said, "This will do."

The next morning Grandfather took the bone, cut off the ends, and drilled finger holes along its length. When he was finished, he handed the flute to Little Fox and nodded for him to try it.

It wasn't a melody but, to the boy, it sounded beautiful.
"The rest is up to you," said Grandfather. "Practice."
And that's just what Little Fox did, every chance he got.

Times grew hard. The rains didn't come, the crops didn't grow, and hunting was poor.

It seemed the Spirits who ruled over the weather didn't care, for it remained dry and the days seemed hotter and longer than ever. With little to eat, the people became bitter and discouraged.

To take his mind off his empty stomach, Little Fox practiced his flute in the shade of a mesquite tree. After a while, he played so sweetly that birds sang along.

One night at the tribal campfire, a brave stood up and said,
"The tribe over the mountain has turned the Spirits against us."
Even though there was no proof of this, many agreed.
Just like that, some began to talk of fighting the other tribe to get even.

The braves began bringing
their spears and war clubs to Grandfather for repair.
Something must be done, Little Fox thought, before my tribe
gives up its peaceful ways. He had an idea and told Grandfather,
who said, "It's worth a try." They laid aside the weapons that had been
brought to them and, instead, worked on the boy's plan.

A few days later, Little Fox sneaked out of the village. Down by the stream, he decorated some of the buzzard feathers, tied them in his hair, and painted his face.

This done, he threw the sack over his shoulder that he and Grandfather had filled, and journeyed over the mountain into the land of the other tribe.

At dusk the soft notes of a flute came floating above the stillness in the other village. Everyone heard it. Some braves reached for their weapons but quickly relaxed under the spell of the beautiful sound.

"Pelli!" shouted a little girl.
This was their word for a kind of bug.
She was pointing at the silly figure
dancing toward them.
To her, the feathers looked like
the antennae of the insect.

As the curious Indians gathered around, the stranger dropped
the pack off his back and began handing out gifts.
To the children he gave animal carvings; to the women, bracelets;
and each man got an arrowhead.

Little Fox told the people that his tribe, in spite of the hardship of no rain, wanted to share what they had with their neighbors, who must also be suffering.

A feast was held in the visitor's honor. Even though there wasn't much to go around, everyone was happy for the first time in a long time. They danced as Pelli played.

As Pelli was about to leave the next morning, the chief asked everyone to put a gift in his sack so there would be presents to give when he got back home.

When the flute was heard again, Pelli was dancing into his own village.
Just as before, the mood of the Indians gathering about him
went from curious to happy as he surprised them with little gifts.
At first only Little Fox's mother and grandfather recognized him.
They shared knowing smiles.

Looking down, the Sun and the Wind spirits
saw how just one boy, Little Fox,
had turned the hearts of the people
from anger to happiness.
This pleased them greatly.

Sun and Wind noticed the Rain spirit wasn't with them. They found him sleeping, shook him awake, and scolded him for ignoring the cries of the people for rain.

The Rain Spirit
grumbled and thundered.
He ground the clouds together,
making rain.

The Indians rejoiced. Their crops were saved. There would be plenty to eat. Since the rain had come with the stranger, they gave him credit. The chief added the word "Koko", which means spirit or deity, to Pelli, making him Kokopelli, the name he has had ever since. To the Indians, the Kokopelli had power for fertility, good crops, and music.

Soon there were other Kokopellis traveling from village to village.
Like Little Fox, each Kokopelli came dancing and playing a flute
to announce his arrival. Kokopellis brought news and carried a sack full of items
to trade. In this way, the tribes learned about each other and lived in peace for
many, many moons. So remember, the next time you see a Kokopelli -
he brings good news to put
a smile in your heart.